Katie Price's
Perfect Ponies

Star Ponies

1 Here Comes the Bride

2 Little Treasures

3 Fancy Dress Ponies

4 Pony Club Weekend

5 The New Best Friend

6 Ponies to the Rescue

7 Star Ponies

www.**kids**at**randomhouse**.co.uk

For fun, games and lots, lots more visit
www.**katiesperfectponies**.co.uk

STAR PONIES
A BANTAM BOOK 978 0 553 82082 9

First published in Great Britain by Bantam,
an imprint of Random House Children's Books
A Random House Group Company

This edition published 2007

1 3 5 7 9 10 8 6 4 2

Copyright © Katie Price, 2007
Katie's Perfect Ponies™ is a trade mark owned by Katie Price

The right of Katie Price to be identified as the author of this work has been asserted
in accordance with the Copyright, Designs and Patents Act 1988.

The Random House Group Limited makes every effort to ensure that the papers used
in its books are made from trees that have been legally sourced from well-managed
and credibly certified forests. Our paper procurement policy can be found at:
www.randomhouse.co.uk/paper.htm

Set in 14/21pt Bembo MT Schoolbook

Bantam Books are published by Random House Children's Books,
61–63 Uxbridge Road, London W5 5SA

www.**kids**at**randomhouse**.co.uk
www.rbooks.co.uk

Addresses for companies within The Random House Group Limited
can be found at: www.randomhouse.co.uk/offices.htm

THE RANDOM HOUSE GROUP Limited Reg. No. 954009
A CIP catalogue record for this book is available from the British Library.

Printed in the UK by CPI Bookmarque, Croydon, CR0 4TD

Katie Price's
Perfect Ponies

Star Ponies

Illustrated by Dynamo Design

Bantam Books

Vicki's Riding School

Vicki

Jess and Rose

Cara and Taffy

Amber and Stella

Sam and Beanz

Mel and Candy

Henrietta and President

Darcy and Duke

Chapter One

"Time to get up," Jess's mum shouted up the stairs.

"Yeah, just a bit longer," Jess mumbled, snuggling under her pink pony duvet so that only a few strands of her thick brown hair were showing. She went back to sleep and carried on dreaming . . .

She galloped up to the fence, tightening her hold on Rose's reins. Then she leaned forward in the saddle and cleared the fence with no problems at all!

"Wicked!"

"Good one!" shouted her friends, waving in the crowd.

*Jess buried her face in Rose's silver mane.
"You're the best pony ever," she told the gorgeous grey Connemara.*

Suddenly her brilliant dream was interrupted again.

"Jessica! Don't make me come up there!"

"I'm up, Mum, chill out!" she shouted back, forcing herself to sit up in bed.

For a minute Jess thought about getting straight back under the covers again. It was cold and still dark outside. But then she looked up at the photo of Rose on her wall and her mood changed immediately. She smiled, remembering her dream.

She had to get up and go to the stables. Rose would be waiting for her.

Jess loved Saturdays – once she'd managed to get up! Spending the whole day at the stables with her best friends, Amber, Sam, Mel, Cara and Darcy, and her beautiful pony, Rose, was the highlight of her week – even if it did mean getting up well early!

Jess had belonged to Vicki's Riding School for nearly two years and she loved it more every day. She'd always been into ponies but there was no way her mum could ever have afforded to buy her one. But one day Jess's mum had got chatting to Amber's mum at the supermarket where she worked and had found out about the stables. The very next day she had taken Jess to meet Vicki. They'd also met beautiful Rose and Jess had fallen in love!

After a few months – in return for Jess's

hard work around the stables – Vicki had given her the special responsibility of looking after Rose *and* agreed to let her have a free weekly riding lesson. At first Jess had been nervous about having her own pony to look after, but Rose was good-natured and patient and now they totally trusted each other.

Joining the stables also meant that Jess had got to know other girls – yard girls like herself, who couldn't afford their own ponies. They were her best friends now!

She'd liked Amber straight away. She was beautiful, with deep, dark eyes and long jet-black hair. Amber was very clever, and brilliant with all the ponies, not just Stella, the stunning Highland pony with the white star blaze that she took special care of. Then there was Sam, the only person who could *always* make Jess laugh. She looked a bit like a clown too, with her messy, spiky ginger hair sticking out all over the place! Sam and her skittish skewbald New Forest cross, Beanz, suited each other perfectly.

There was Mel and Cara too. They were best friends, just like Jess and Amber, but as different as chalk and cheese! Mel was loud, feisty and tough. She and her gorgeous chestnut Arab pony, Candy, were amazing to watch, and were definitely the best jumpers in the school. Cara and her palomino Welsh pony, Taffy, were the complete opposite. Taffy was sturdy, calm and reliable, but he obviously adored his shy, blonde-haired mistress as much as she loved him.

Jess smiled, still thinking of them all, until suddenly she realized she'd been daydreaming for *ages*. "Argh!" she shouted, quickly pulling on her jodhpurs. She was in a rush but she still wanted to try and look glam, so she hunted around for her favourite pink jumper. Jess knew Sam and Mel didn't mind what they looked like at the stables, as long as they were warm and comfortable. But Jess wanted to be like Vicki, who always looked gorgeous, no matter what job she was doing in the riding school – even if she was tidying the muck heap!

Jess quickly brushed her hair, then legged it downstairs and into the kitchen. She was starving as well as late!

"About time," snapped her mum. "Don't you think I've got more important things to do than spend an hour every weekend dragging your lazy bum out of bed? Amber's already called round. I told her to go on without you."

They had the same argument every Saturday because Jess was so bad at getting up! She only half listened to her mum telling her off as she put two pieces of bread in the toaster and poured some orange juice. "I'm sorry, Mum," she said, gulping the juice. "I promise I'll get up straight away next week."

"I'll believe that when I see it," Jess's mum said, with a smile now. "Your wellies are by the door,"

she told her. "Don't put them on till you're outside, they're muddy."

"OK," Jess mumbled, folding one slice of the toast in half and putting it in her mouth all at once. She grabbed the other piece, kissed her mum goodbye and ran to the front door. Sitting down on the step, she pulled on her wellies, reached in to grab her coat, then ran

down the road. She'd only been gone a couple of minutes when she remembered that she'd left her second piece of toast on the carpet by the front door. Jess grinned, hoping her mum didn't stand on it. Then she really would be in trouble!

Jess ran all the way to the stables. As she rushed up the drive, she bumped into Mel.

"Hey, babe," Jess said as she slowed down to walk with her friend. Even though Jess always seemed confident – the yard girls usually looked on her as their leader – she was secretly quite jealous of Mel. She was really pretty, with soft brown eyes and dark curly hair *and* she was a brilliant horsewoman. She always seemed so cool and brave.

Mel grinned at Jess. "Did you have to rush again?" she laughed, looking at her friend's flushed face.

"Yep," Jess giggled. "I just love my bed too much."

"I bet your—" Mel started to say. But she stopped suddenly at the sight of a very cross-looking Vicki standing at the entrance to the stables.

9

"Uh-oh," mumbled Mel quietly. "I don't like the look of this."

Vicki was stunning as well as a really nice person. All the girls loved and looked up to her. She was an amazing rider and had won loads of competitions on Jelly, her Irish-cross thoroughbred. *And* she ran the riding school with only Susie, her nineteen-year-old assistant, and the yard girls to help her. She always made sure that the ponies and horses were happy and well looked after. Now, Vicki's silver-grey eyes were looking daggers at Jess and Mel and she was running her hand through her thick dark hair. She was definitely not pleased and both girls knew it.

"Jess, Mel," she snapped as they got closer. "I'm not impressed. I don't know what you think this is. One or both of you is late every Saturday at the moment. If you don't take your positions here more seriously,

10

I'll have to think carefully about whether
Rose and Candy have the right girls looking
after them."

Jess gasped with shock and she felt Mel do
the same. The thought of not having Rose
in her life any more was just so awful, she
wanted to cry.

"Sorry, Vicki," Mel said quickly.

"Yeah, we're really sorry," Jess added.

"Well, being *sorry* doesn't get Rose and Candy's stables mucked out or them tacked ready for lessons, does it?" Vicki asked sharply.

They'd never seen Vicki like this before. Not even with snotty Henrietta Reece-Thomas, one of the girls who kept her pony at livery and who caused as much trouble for Vicki and her helpers as she could. Totally shocked, the girls looked at each other, puzzled, before putting their heads down and bombing it over to the stables.

Jess and Mel stormed through their morning duties, hardly speaking to the other yard girls. Sam, Amber and Cara wondered what had made their normally lively friends so quiet. After the ponies were groomed and tacked, the girls clipped lead ropes onto their headcollars and led them outside, walking on the left-hand side of the ponies, just as Vicki had taught them.

As they walked over to the indoor school, sensitive Cara asked, "Melly, what's wrong? You're so quiet. Has something happened?"

Jess and Mel told the girls what had happened on their way in that morning. The others were as surprised as they were.

"Wonder what can have put Vicki in such a mood?" asked Sam.

"Mmm," Amber said thoughtfully. "She snapped at me during my lesson this week too."

"I know we were a bit late," Jess admitted, "but we've never been too late to get ready for lessons."

"And you work well hard when you're here," Amber added.

Cara never let the girls moan for long. "Don't, guys," she said. "Vicki's amazing, you know that. If it wasn't for her we'd never have these gorgeous ponies." She turned and hugged Taffy round his creamy golden neck.

"You're right, as usual, Car," Jess agreed. "Everybody's allowed a bad week."

But she was still worried. Jess thought Vicki was fab . . . What could be making her behave like this?

Chapter Two

Phew, lessons are nearly over, Jess thought as she led little Ben round the outdoor school on Carol. Carol was the newest pony at the stables, a mischievous Shetland that Vicki had bought just a month ago.

Jess had been trying all morning to get Ben to remember to sit up straight. She knew that there should be a straight line from Carol's mouth, along her reins and through his hands to his elbows. This was the only way to keep proper contact with the pony's mouth, and Jess knew how important it was to learn early on. She was just about to remind him again, when Vicki got there first.

"How many times do I have to tell you, Ben? Back straight! You look like a sack of potatoes," she snapped at the little boy.

Jess and Mel looked at each other. Even Susie, Vicki's assistant, seemed surprised by Vicki's outburst and looked up.

Just then, Flora's old, frayed lead rope snapped off in Cara's hand. Normally Vicki laughed when things like this happened. But not today. Today she looked like she was going to explode.

Poor Ben started to cry and Jess, who loved all the Saturday kids, even naughty Ben and his naughtier twin brother, Bill, tried to calm him down.

So everybody was relieved when, at that moment, a little blue car came zooming into the yard and distracted Vicki. A beautiful blonde-haired woman stepped out and started looking around.

"Wonder who that is," Mel said to Sam.

"She's gorgeous."

"Hellooo," the woman called, crossing the yard towards the outdoor school.

At first Vicki looked annoyed that someone was interrupting her class but then, suddenly, a smile broke out across her face for the first time that day.

She ran over to the woman and hugged her. They chatted for a minute and then started vto walk towards Vicki's office.

"Susie! Girls!" Vicki shouted over her shoulder. "Can you finish up here while I talk to Helen?"

The girls were even more shocked. Vicki hated missing lessons. When she'd taken a day off last year to be a bridesmaid, she'd worried about it for weeks before. What was going on?

With lessons over and the ponies tired from the morning's hard work, Jess and the rest of the girls took them back to the stables to brush them down.

Jess had been in such a rush and so upset about Vicki earlier, she'd not made as much fuss of Rose as normal when she'd tacked her up. She wanted to make it up to her now. She grabbed the pink tack box, which she'd bought herself and decorated with pony stickers and ribbons.

She talked to Rose softly as she untacked

her and spent a long time brushing her
down to remove all the sweat from the
morning's hard work. By the time she'd
finished, Rose's silver coat was shimmering.

But Jess was still thinking about Vicki.
What if she did decide to take Rose away
from her? Jess didn't know what she'd do.

Rose's ears pricked up. She sensed that

19

her mistress was worried, so she rubbed her beautiful grey muzzle against Jess's tummy to try and make her feel better.

Jess held out a chunk of carrot in the palm of her hand and Rose munched it greedily.

"You're the best, babe," she told the pony. But tears came into her eyes as she thought about Vicki's threat again. "What would I do without you?"

After all the girls had finished grooming and had some lunch, they led the ponies over to the meadow so they could chill out.

Chilling out wasn't what they had in mind though! As soon as their lead ropes were unclipped, the ponies galloped off, chasing around wildly. They loved being part of a big gang of friends. They got on almost as well as the girls did and had lots of fun together.

The five friends hung around for a while watching their ponies and smiling proudly.

Graceful Rose, skittish Beanz, headstrong Candy, steady Stella and laid-back Taffy really did match their owners perfectly.

As the girls turned to go, Sam pulled the five-bar gate shut. But as she did so, the catch broke off and fell onto the grass.

"Oh, no!" Sam groaned. "Bags not telling Vicki. She'll bite my head off!"

"Let's all go and tell her together," Jess said, sighing. Normally she'd have jumped at any chance to go and talk to Vicki, but she had to agree with Sam – today was *so* not a good day to have to tell her that something else had broken.

"Come on, guys," Cara smiled. "It's not as if Sammy did it on purpose. It's well old and needed replacing anyway. Vicki will understand."

Amber was thinking about the animals as usual. "One of us should stay here. We can't leave the gate swinging open or the ponies will get out."

"Good thinking, Am," smiled Mel, giving her a hug. "I'll stay. None of them will dare try and get past me!"

The rest of the girls walked slowly in the direction of Vicki's office. But soon they saw her coming out and walking towards them.

"Umm . . . Maybe we should have fought Mel to see who got to stay with the ponies." Sam giggled nervously, joking as usual.

As they got closer, they were surprised to see that the frown that had been on Vicki's face all morning had disappeared. She was smiling, but she did look a bit flustered.

"Girls," she called, "I'm so glad you're here. I was just coming to find you. I owe you a serious apology for my behaviour."

Jess ran up to Vicki and gave her a massive hug. "You do still want us to work at the stables, don't you?" she asked. "You're not going to take the ponies off us?"

Vicki hugged her back. "Of course I won't, sweetheart!" she exclaimed. "What gave you that idea? I know I've been moody, but I don't know what I'd do without you all."

"Good!" Sam laughed. "Then maybe now's the time to tell you that the catch on the five-bar gate to the pony meadow is broken."

Vicki grinned and rolled her eyes. "Well, that's part of why I've been in such a mood – and I'll explain in a bit. But first, I've got some news . . ."

Four excited faces looked up at her.

"You know the lady who arrived during lessons today?"

"She was gorgeous," breathed Cara. "She looked like a model." The rest of them nodded in agreement.

"Well, we went to school together. And she works behind the camera, not in front of it — for the production company that makes the TV show, *Feelings*," Vicki told them. "Have you heard of it?"

"*Yes!* I love that programme!" shouted Amber. "I watch it every week."

"Well, Helen's asked for my help with an episode . . ." Vicki stopped and smiled at them all. "Girls . . . our ponies are going to be TV stars!"

Chapter Three

"Wow!" they all shouted.

"That's amazing!" whooped Sam, chucking the broken catch of the gate up in the air.

"What's amazing?" asked Darcy, coming over. Jess liked Darcy a lot. She didn't see as much of her as she did Amber, Sam, Mel and Cara, because she went to a private school out of town and kept her stunning dark bay pony, Duke, in livery.

But the more time she spent with her, the more Jess saw that Darcy was really down to earth and nothing at all like a couple of the other livery girls, Henrietta Reece-Thomas and her friend Camilla Worthington.

Vicki quickly told Darcy what she'd told the others.

"So what does this mean, Vicki?" asked Jess. She'd already started thinking how proud she'd be of Rose, if she was picked to be on TV.

But Vicki was, as always, thinking of the ponies. "I suppose Mel's waiting at the meadow, if the gate's broken?" she asked hopefully.

Sam nodded.

Vicki smiled. "Let's walk over together so I can tell you all at the same time," she suggested, grabbing some rope and starting off towards the meadow.

"This sounds wicked!" Jess whispered excitedly to Amber as they followed Vicki.

Half an hour later, the girls were even more excited!

Vicki had told them that the episode of *Feelings* included one of the most important male characters – a really gorgeous, famous actor – having his first riding lesson. Jess knew exactly who Vicki meant. Her mum loved him!

The episode was on a really tight filming schedule and the film crew had a big problem. The stables they'd planned to use and had checked out a month ago had been damaged by a fire the day before. Nothing too serious, and no ponies or horses had been hurt, but the director had to find a different stables – quickly! Helen had remembered about Vicki and had driven over straight away to see what her old friend thought about them using her riding school!

"Wow, Vicki," Darcy said. "So you said yes?"

"No . . ." Vicki shook her head. "I told Helen I'd have to think about it. I've got to let her know by the end of the day."

"What!" shrieked Mel and Sam at exactly the same time.

Cara looked across at Vicki and asked softly, "Why don't you want to do it, Vicki?"

"Because it's going to be really disruptive, Cara," she told her. "It has to be filmed next weekend, so the crew are going to be in and out of the stables every day this week. They've got to set up the lighting and the sound and get the cast used to being around the ponies and the ponies used to them. *And* I've still got a yard to run."

Jess was surprised. She hadn't realized how much work was involved in making a short TV programme. She'd thought everyone would just turn up on the day with cameras and start filming. "We'll help as much as we can, you know." She smiled shyly.

31

The rest of the girls nodded.

"I'll get out of netball and hockey practice after school this week if I can, too," said Darcy.

"Thanks, babe. That's really sweet of you – of all of you – and I will have to take you up on it if I agree," Vicki said.

"So, if we promise to be extra-helpful this week, you'll say yes?" asked Sam cheekily.

Vicki grinned at the freckly face in front of her. "Actually, there's a much bigger reason to say yes — and it's why I've been so moody lately."

"Is it anything serious, Vicki?" asked Amber thoughtfully.

"Well, I suppose you've noticed how shabby things are looking round here," Vicki said.

Sam looked over at the five-bar gate, now held together with the length of rope that Vicki had brought across from the yard. "No! Not at all," she laughed.

"It's quite serious though, Sam," Vicki said, frowning. "I've lost a couple of the Saturday kids. Their parents took them to those new Primrose Stables in the next village because they were 'much smarter'."

"Well, that's their stupid loss," hot-headed Mel interrupted.

"Maybe," said Vicki. "But I can't help

thinking they're right: things *are* too scruffy. It's not just gates and lead ropes. The grooming kits and tack all need replacing, and everywhere needs whitewashing, but I just can't afford it at the moment. You girls did an amazing job with the fundraising at Christmas, but the school still had to spend quite a lot of money on Carol."

"Maybe we could do some more fundraising?" Cara suggested nervously.

Vicki smiled, but Jess was wondering what this had to do with the filming. Was Vicki embarrassed about the school being on TV? She didn't understand. Vicki's Riding School might not be the "smartest" stables, but she loved it just the way it was. "Maybe having the school on telly will make loads of people want to join," she said excitedly.

"Ooh, yes," agreed Amber.

Vicki smiled again. "I hadn't thought of that, but we would be mentioned in the credits, I suppose. But, no, it's not really to do with having the school on TV. It's that they'll be paying us for letting them use the stables. That will certainly come in handy! And they'll paint the place and get the set carpenters to repair lots of the broken doors and fences."

"Do it, then, Vicki! Beanz might be famous!" Sam shrieked.

"Well . . ." Vicki paused for a moment. "It'd be daft not to really. And Beanz *might* be famous, Sam. They're using the horses from the first stables they chose for the main characters cos they've got used to each other. But they'd like to use a few of our ponies for the extras to lead on camera."

The girls cheered excitedly.

Vicki stood up. "Right then, if you're all happy, I'd better go and tell Helen yes!"

Later, when all the other chores were done, Jess and her friends decided to tuck the ponies up for the night. Even though it was only four o'clock, it was getting dark and they'd had a long day. The others were gossiping happily about how brilliant the next week would be. But Jess was quiet and thinking hard.

She was planning all the extra-special grooming she was going to do for Rose over the next week, to make sure she'd definitely get her chance to be famous. Jess had some ribbon that she'd been saving for something special. Rose loved being dressed up so Jess thought she would wrap the ribbon round her pony's browband to make her look even prettier. It was pink and would go perfectly with her silver mane.

Then Jess's thoughts were interrupted by a sound she hated but knew well – Henrietta Reece-Thomas's voice! The snotty livery girl had overheard the girls' conversation.

"I suppose this means you've heard the news too?" she snapped, flicking her blonde hair. "Vicki's already told me."

"Oh, good," snapped Mel – she got the most wound up by Henrietta. "Then we all know, so we don't have stand here and talk to you about it." And she started to lead Candy into her stable.

But Henrietta wasn't finished. "Well, I wouldn't have thought *you* needed to talk about it at all," she said snootily. "As if any of you common losers or your borrowed old nags will get the chance to be on TV. You've not got a look-in with me and Camilla around." Camilla was Henrietta's best friend and just as stuck up as her. "They'll obviously want people with *class*."

Mel squared up to Henrietta.

"Actually, Henrietta," Vicki interrupted quickly, coming out of her office, "they don't want any *people* at all. I've just spoken to Helen and it's definitely the ponies that will be the stars, not us. The cast is sorted. And we don't know which ponies the director will want to use until Monday."

"There's not much competition really though, is there?" whispered Henrietta to

Mel and Jess. "They're bound to choose a beautiful Appaloosa like President over your second-hand nags."

If Vicki heard the snide comment, she ignored it. "The good news is, I *did* get all you girls special permission to watch the filming next weekend as long as you're on hand to help." The girls cheered! "But with this attitude from you, Henrietta, I will have to think carefully about whether I want you representing my school at all." And with that, Vicki turned and walked back into her office, leaving Henrietta red in the face and the other girls smiling.

Jess watched Vicki leave. She turned to the other yard girls, grinning excitedly. "She's so cool! And this is going to be so much fun!"

Chapter Four

Jess spent hours every day after school grooming Rose till she shone. She washed her tail with special horse shampoo and Vicki showed her how to clip Rose's mane, saying, "Every girl needs to look her best!" *All* the yard girls spent ages with their ponies and they were *so* excited!

Members of the film crew had been carrying lots of tools and equipment to and fro all week. They looked quite scary – dressed in black and shouting – but they'd actually been really nice. Because of them, the stables looked different already! They wanted to make sure that everything looked

perfect on camera so they'd done loads of
work around the place. They'd fixed the
chipped wood and then painted the doors
of all the stables, plus the tack room and
Vicki's office, and they'd fixed the locks on

them. They'd repaired the fence all around the pony meadow and put a whole new lock on the five-bar gate. One of the crew had even weeded in between the cobbles in the yard!

Darcy had a brainwave. "I just saw one of the men whitewashing and painting the inside walls of the tack room," she said excitedly.

"Why's a bit of painting so exciting?" asked Mel sarcastically.

"OK, moody bum." Darcy smiled, pretending to hit her. "I just thought that maybe if he had any paint spare after all the work was done *and* we asked nicely, he might give it to us so we can all do the insides of our ponies' stables. *They* look tatty too, but because they won't be shown on TV, they're not being tidied up."

"That's such a good idea, Darcy," Cara cried.

"Yep," agreed Amber. *"And* it will give us something to do when all the excitement of this week is over."

"Let's definitely ask," Jess said, wondering if she'd be able to get any pink paint!

The director of *Feelings,* Carl, had been to the stables on Monday afternoon to check it out – and look at all the ponies. Jess had felt very nervous in front of him. He had long

dark hair pulled back into a ponytail and big, black sunglasses even though it was winter! Jess thought he looked brilliant – like a film star – but gobby Mel wasn't a fan.

"He looks like a poser,"

she said loudly. "I'm not bothered if Candy doesn't get picked to be on TV. I don't want her being bossed around by that stupid man."

Henrietta, who was hanging around as near to Carl as possible, overheard their conversation. "Keep telling yourself that if it makes you feel better. Your grubby old nag would never get picked over the much classier ponies in the stables anyway," she said nastily.

Even though she was playing it cool, Jess knew that Henrietta was trying just as hard to make sure that President was picked for *Feelings*. She'd even spent time grooming President herself – something Jess had never seen her do before. Sam had nearly fainted with shock when she saw Henrietta with a dandy brush in her hand!

Camilla had tried to groom her pony, Cleopatra, too, but she was a rubbish horsewoman and did stupid things like brushing Cleo roughly under her tummy. The poor pony hated it and would pull away impatiently from Camilla, tossing her head. But Camilla never bothered to learn what Cleo liked and didn't like. She never spent any time just petting and talking to her pony. Camilla was living proof that you shouldn't bother buying a posh pony if you can't ride or look after it properly.

After only half an hour, Camilla gave up trying to keep Cleo still and Henrietta was bored. Then they came and ordered Jess and Amber, who were on livery duty, to finish what they'd started.

Amber was giving Henrietta's pony some much-needed attention. "President *is* gorgeous," she said, stroking his beautiful grey mane. "I know we always say it, but he deserves somebody *sooo* much better than Henrietta."

"Yep," agreed Jess. "He's lovely. He

just needs some TLC." She stopped and frowned, thinking about the two livery girls. "But I think I feel more sorry for Cleo. President's lovely and well too good for Snotty Knickers, but with the right owner, Cleo'd be an amazing pony. As it is, nobody wants to go near her because she's so much trouble!"

With Jess and Amber's help, President, and even stubborn Cleo, had looked beautiful on Monday afternoon when Carl arrived. He told Vicki that he'd need eight ponies for a scene. They'd be led across the yard towards the pony meadow by eight young actresses.

First Carl had paced up and down the yard, then outside the stables, looking over the top of his sunglasses and then glancing

down to make notes. The girls huddled together, all behaving differently. Jess stood still, winding her thick brown hair round her finger. Cara was almost crying with nerves. Amber and Darcy stood fidgeting but said nothing; Sam kept trying to make funny comments about what Carl might be writing; but only Mel, who was trying to pretend she wasn't bothered by what was going on, laughed.

As it turned out, none of the girls needed to worry! Carl chose Rose, Stella, Beanz, Candy, Taffy, Duke, President and Cleopatra as the ponies for his shoot. Jess and her friends jumped for joy and even Mel gave Jess a high-five! Jess was so happy! Not only was Rose going to get her chance to be a star, but all her friends' ponies were too. Nobody would be left out!

As soon as Carl had made his announcement, Vicki quickly tried to advise him against using Cleo at all. "Really," she said in a low voice to stop the girls overhearing, "she's *very* risky. Not at all well trained. I had problems with her and a weak rider just a couple of months ago. It could be really dangerous."

Jess overheard and cringed. She knew the weak rider Vicki was talking about was Lauren, a friend Jess had brought into the stables who'd turned out to be a real cow.

Carl was getting stroppy. "Look, I want to use this pony, darling," he said, pushing his sunglasses up on top of his head and putting one hand on his hip. "I want her at the front of the shot. She's gorgeous. But," he threatened, "I *can* look elsewhere for a new stableful of ponies. One that doesn't involve my team having to do so much tidying up . . ."

Jess didn't really believe this – she'd heard loads of the cast and crew saying how great it was that Helen had managed to find such

a nice place at short notice. Carl really
needed to get the episode filmed. But she
also knew how much the stables needed this
clean-up and the bit of money they'd get at
the end of it. So she understood why Vicki
kept her mouth shut about Cleo, just saying,

"Well . . . OK, but I have to be around the whole time Cleo's being used," before walking away, shaking her head.

Mel and Sam were really cool around the film crew and were even calm when the cast arrived on Wednesday afternoon to rehearse. Jess and Amber couldn't stop giggling and Cara wouldn't speak, just going bright red every time she passed somebody she didn't know.

Jess really wanted to get an autograph from Will, the main actor, for her mum. Normally she was fine talking to strangers, but he was so famous, she was too shy to speak to him.

"I'll come with you and ask," said Mel confidently. "He's just a person, not an alien!"

"No, but he is *really* good looking," Cara said, blushing.

"Isn't he a bit old for you, Car?" Mel

teased, making their shy friend go an even darker shade of red.

He *was* good looking, with dark hair and blue eyes. He wore trendy clothes and a green cap. Jess had seen Henrietta and Camilla trying to suck up to him already, which put her off wanting to go and speak to him in case she looked as stupid as they did. But she really wanted to surprise her mum with the autograph, so she followed Mel over to him.

"Excuse me, Will, I'm Mel and this is Jess," Mel said confidently. "We're so pleased to meet you. Jess's mum is a really big fan of yours. Do you think you'd be able to sign this for her?" And she handed him the piece of pink card that Jess had got ready.

"Course. No problem, girls," he said,
smiling at them as he signed it. "Anything
for the ladies and their ponies who've saved
the day!" And he gave them both a kiss on
the cheek.

Even Mel was charmed by him and she
blushed as they walked back over to the rest
of the girls.

"Ooh, Mel," Darcy teased. "Now *you're*
all red. Even redder than Cara!"

Before Mel could retort, Henrietta got in with her usual nasty comment. "Of course she's red. I'd be red if I'd been showing off to a famous actor."

"Oh shut up, Henrietta," Amber shouted. "We saw you and Camilla all over him before."

"That's not true," Camilla butted in. "We were having a civilized conversation – something *you* wouldn't know about. Anyway, Mummy knows him. Well . . . she knows his aunty. She was going to try and get me in *Feelings* but I couldn't be bothered and I thought it would be nice for Cleo to be the star attraction on Saturday."

Chapter Five

Saturday morning dawned bright and clear.
Jess couldn't wait for filming to begin. As
soon as morning lessons were over, the girls
stuffed their faces with the sandwiches and
crisps they'd brought with them. Normally
they swapped food and drink and chatted
over lunch, but today the tack room was
almost silent. Even Sam was quieter than
normal! They were all nervous and just
wanted to get back to their ponies to give
them one last brush down before their star
performances.

Jess went back to Rose, who was tethered
to the ring in her stable, and quickly

brushed the final bits of dirt out of her silver coat and tail. "I'm going to be so proud of you, babe," she whispered.

Amber appeared outside Rose's stable. "I just said the same to Stella," she giggled. "It's going to be so weird when we see them on TV."

Carl wanted to film the group scenes first, so that the young actresses wouldn't be kept hanging around all day. The ponies were going to be used straight away!

When Helen came to call the ponies into the yard, she was struggling with a big box. After she'd put it carefully on the ground, she pulled out a brand-new headcollar and lead rope for each of the ponies!

"Wow!" Amber cried. "These are so posh and shiny – they'll look amazing on camera."

"Well, that's the idea." Helen smiled. "But think of them as a thank you from

us to you for letting us borrow your lovely ponies."

"What?!" gasped Cara. "You mean we can keep them?"

"Of course," Helen said. "Why don't you use them as your special occasion ones or something?"

And this really *was* a special occasion! As Helen led the girls and their newly tacked-up ponies to the yard, Jess gasped. The spotless yard was brightly lit by the early-afternoon sun, the new paint dazzling.

There were loads of cameras and lights – it looked just like she'd imagined a real film set. She felt like she could almost be a star herself!

But she was brought back down to earth by Rose pulling on her lead rope. Her pony was slightly spooked by the amount of equipment and people in her way so Jess spoke soothingly to her and stroked her head. Behind her, she heard Amber do the same for Stella and Darcy for Duke.

Jess was worried about Beanz and Cleo. They were really frisky and wouldn't like all this unusual stuff going on around them.

She knew Sam would be OK controlling Beanz. She just hoped that Vicki would remember her promise to Carl and help out with Cleo. Camilla would definitely need a hand with her skittish pony.

In fact it was Vicki who led Cleo over from the stables, talking softly into her ear and stroking her head exactly as she had taught Jess to do with Rose.

"OK," shouted Carl, interrupting Jess's thoughts. "Let's get going!"

Jess led Rose over to Sophie, the actress she was going to be filmed with. She was very nice and Jess was pleased that she'd taken the trouble to come over and get to know Rose during the week. But she couldn't help feeling jealous as she handed Rose over to her. "Love you, babe! Good luck!" she whispered under her breath,

Then came Carl's voice, "Silence please! Episode two three five. Scene twenty-three.

Take one. Lights, camera, action!"

Everybody hushed. Even Henrietta and Camilla were quiet! Jess joined Amber behind some cameras and grabbed hold of her hand nervously.

Cara crept up to join them too. "I feel as scared as if I was being filmed!" she whispered, biting her lip.

The eight girls leading Rose, Stella, Beanz, Candy, Taffy, Duke, President and Cleopatra knew exactly what to do, and the stable girls and Darcy watched closely. They'd practised the scene quite a few times during the week. Vicki had taught them all to lead correctly so it looked like they really belonged to the riding school – from the left-hand side, holding the lead rein with their right hand near the headcollar and the other end off the ground with their left hand.

The actresses looked great – all dressed in different colours, and wearing hard hats and gloves for safety. They walked across the yard, pretending they were all really good friends.

I'd love to be on TV, Jess thought, *but I'm well glad that I can do this for real.* The other yard girls had joined Jess, Amber and Cara and felt exactly the same.

"It's like a film of us!" said Mel softly.

"Yeah. It's weird though," Darcy whispered back. "I don't like this other girl pretending she's Duke's owner. I—"

She stopped. Carl had turned round and was looking daggers at them. Henrietta and Camilla were smiling snidely, pleased that they'd been caught out talking. *Honestly,* Jess thought, *I don't know why they've got such a problem with us. We always try and be nice and we look after their ponies so well for them.*

At first it was very exciting being on set, but after an hour of watching the same thing over and over again, the girls were growing bored. It looked like the ponies were too. Beanz was jigging up and down and Cleo was tossing her head impatiently. Carl needed to shoot the same scene from lots of different angles so he could cut and edit it later in the studio to look exactly how he wanted. The eight girls and the ponies had now made the journey across the yard towards the meadow so many times that Jess had lost count.

Henrietta and Camilla had got bored ages ago and wandered off so Carl couldn't hear them. Jess could hear them whispering though. They were making nasty comments about all the actresses. Henrietta really was a cow.

Vicki hurried over to the yard girls with a frown on her gorgeous face. "Girls, I'm worried about the ponies," she said softly, running a hand through her hair. "They're getting impatient  and frisky, especially Beanz and Cleo."

"I know," said Sam, "I was just thinking that Beanz needs a break. I'm scared he's going to bolt if they go on much longer."

"Yes," agreed Amber. "And Carli, the girl he's with, is starting to look a bit nervous."

Carli *did* look nervous. She shook her long blonde hair out of her face and looked over at Sam, frowning.

"The brown-haired girl with Cleo doesn't look like a very strong horsewomen either," worried Cara. "You know what Cleo's like. It makes me really nervous. Look what happened when she bolted with Lauren."

"Hmmm," thought Vicki out loud. "I'll go and speak to Helen about them getting a break before there's an accident and something gets broken – or worse, somebody gets hurt."

"Good idea," said Mel. "We need money for the stables, not to pay for everything Cleo's damaged during the filming!"

"Oh, I'm sure she just needs a break," Cara said kindly. "She'll be fine."

But maybe Cara had spoken too soon . . .

Chapter Six

Just after Vicki left to find Helen, there was another sudden hush and Carl's voice shouted once again, "Lights, camera, action! Scene twenty-three. Take fourteen."

The actresses moved into position as usual, but Cleo, who was at the front of the group, was starting to get really fed up. She tossed her head and pulled away from Katie, the girl leading her. Katie *had* ridden before, but Cleo was scary when she wanted to be and Katie was panicking. Trying to keep control, she pulled harder on the Arab pony's reins but this just made Cleo angrier. At the same time a camera assistant held

a big furry boom microphone out in front
of the pony so he could pick up the "real"
noises, and Cleo became seriously spooked.

Jess noticed what was happening at once.
"Oh, no!" she shouted. "Cleo doesn't like
that mike one bit – she's going to bolt!"
And without a thought for the filming or
everyone's eyes on her, she legged it round
the yard towards the wild-eyed pony, who
was now stamping and snorting. Jess was

careful not to run in front of her, but caught hold of Cleo's lead rope just as poor Katie lost control and dropped it completely.

Jess ignored the noise and chaos around her and tried to calm the beautiful pony down. She walked her away from all the strange people and equipment and talked softly to her even though *she* was scared of Cleo too and her heart was thumping hard. All around her the noise seemed to be getting louder – she hoped that one of her friends would get Vicki quickly, but until then she just kept talking and held on tightly to Cleo.

The rest of the ponies were upset now too. They'd all started to whinny and toss their heads. A few of the young actresses started to cry as they struggled to keep them under control. Then, to make things worse, Carl was starting to shout!

"What on earth's going on?" he barked, not moving from his director's chair. "Can't one of you girls sort these stupid animals out? Isn't that why you've been hanging around all day?"

Mel, Amber, Sam, Cara and Darcy were already taking their ponies from the girls, so Mel looked daggers at him, then called back over her shoulder, "Henrietta, Camilla! Come on! We need you too."

Jess looked up, relieved to hear Mel's voice. Probably for the first and last time she was pleased to see the snotty livery girls coming towards her too! But she suddenly realized that, in the middle of all the panic, nobody had checked that Katie was OK.

73

Jess looked around the yard, only half concentrating in case Cleo started up again. She couldn't see Katie anywhere!

Cleo sensed that Jess was worried, and as the yard girls ran up to help, the pony began to get spooked again – her sensitive ears pricked up and the whites of her eyes were starting to show. There were just too many people stressing and running about. Jess was really panicking now.

Then came the voice she trusted so much: "Katie! Get up! Now!" But this was not Vicki's usual calming tone.

Jess suddenly realized what Vicki was looking at: Katie was crouched down on the ground, terrified. She was sobbing and hiding her head in her hands . . . right in the firing line of Cleo's back legs.

Jess knew this was the most dangerous thing Katie could possibly do. The pony had no idea what was behind her – she was just scared, and her first instinct would be to kick out and gallop off as fast as she could.

"Katie!" Jess yelled. "Do what Vicki said – get up now and move away quickly! I don't know if I can keep Cleo under control much longer!"

Vicki walked slowly across towards Katie, talking calmly to Cleo to try to make her understand who it was behind her. As soon as she reached the terrified girl, she grabbed her by the arm, pulling her up roughly. "You'll get kicked in the head, you silly girl," she said angrily.

"Move!" But Vicki's advice came too late.

Katie cried out in panic, but didn't move fast enough.

Cleo heard the frightened shout behind her, and what was more she could see the rest of her friends being led away by their mistresses and she wanted to follow them. Straining against her lead rope, she kicked out.

Immediately Jess heard poor Katie scream with pain. She was too scared to look. *Please let her be OK*. Please, she thought. But when she had Cleo under control again, she glanced round. Vicki was crouched down checking on Katie, who was lying on the ground. Her long brown hair was covering her face and, below her knee, blood was seeping through her jodhpurs.

"It's OK, babe, don't worry," Vicki was telling Katie, her soft voice calm again. "You'll be fine. I don't think anything's broken.

Just lie still and I'll get someone to have a
look at you." She got to her feet and turned
to Jess. "Katie's going to be OK. You've done
amazingly – now let me take over."

"I'm so glad
you're here,"
was all Jess
could say, before
passing Cleo's
lead rope over and
bursting into tears.

"Right," Vicki said,
looking stern and giving
directions. "Jessie, honey, if you're OK, just
stay with Katie for a moment. I'll take Cleo,
and the rest of you girls, get your ponies
back to the stables: we need to calm them
down – and Camilla" – she raised her voice
a little, her beautiful grey eyes piercing into
the girl – "for God's sake do something
useful. Jess has looked after your pony long
enough: now look after hers. Get Rose back
with the others instead of just standing there."

All the girls did exactly as she asked. But
Vicki wasn't finished! "Helen!" she called.

"Get your first aider to check on Katie. I don't think anything's broken, but she might need stitches in that leg." Helen nodded, and went off across the yard.

Next, Vicki turned on Carl. "Surely you could see that the ponies were acting up? I told you Cleopatra was too wild to be handled by somebody so inexperienced, and shoving a big piece of equipment in her face before bawling at my girls just made it ten times worse. Honestly!" And with that she led Cleopatra away to join the rest of her ponies.

Jess waited till the first aider had looked at Katie, then followed Vicki and her friends over to the stables. She was shaking and her heart was still pounding, so she walked very slowly to Rose's stable, where Camilla had tied her up.

Jess calmed down straight away at the sight of Rose. When she heard her mistress's footsteps, Rose lifted her head and whinnied

softly, as if she was
saying hello. Jess
opened the stable
door and hugged the
Connemara round
the neck, breathing
in Rose's sweet smell
and feeling better all
the time. "You were
amazing, Rosie," she

whispered. "Definitely the most beautiful
pony on TV." And Rose pulled herself free
and nudged Jess gently in the tummy as if to
say, *I know!*

"What do you think we should do now?"
asked Cara nervously as she filled up Taffy's
water bucket outside. "Do we just tether the
ponies in their stables and leave them?"

"Not sure, Car," replied Darcy, arriving at
that moment from Duke's stable. "But Vicki's
on the case, so I'm sure she'll let us know."

"Yep," chuckled Mel. "She was wicked just then!"

The others laughed.

"Did you see the look on Carl's face when Vicki blasted him?" asked Amber, grinning.

"I know," smiled Cara. "She's so beautiful that nobody ever expects her to be so fierce!"

"Same as Cleo!" joked Sam. "Honestly, she's a maniac!"

Darcy walked along the row of stables, giving each pony a mint. They all munched away happily. "I hope poor Katie's OK though," she said as she reached Taffy's stable at the end of the row.

"Me too," replied Jess. "I can't stop thinking about her. It looked really bad."

"Poor her," said Cara sympathetically. "I bet it's very painful."

"Well" – Henrietta's snooty voice cut through Cara's soft, caring one – "it's her own fault for being so stupid. I mean, even you idiots know never to go behind a pony. It's the first thing you're told."

"Katie's not to blame, Henrietta," Amber snapped. "Cleo's hard to handle at the best of times and spooks easily. You know that."

Camilla shot Amber and the rest of the girls a nasty look, as though they were total scum. She did know how hard Cleo was to handle and either struggled with her herself or just ignored her a lot of the time. But she kept her mouth shut.

Henrietta didn't give up though. "Excuses. That stage school girl obviously wasn't up to the part. It's not even like she had to ride a horse – *anybody* can lead one."

From the corner of her eye, Jess could see Mel getting ready to square up to Snooty Knickers. But Henrietta carried on.

"I mean, it's not even like she's good

looking. I thought TV stars were supposed to be pretty."

That was it. Now Jess had had enough! She moved away from the stables so the ponies wouldn't panic and got up in Henrietta's face. "You total cow!" she said. "Don't pretend that you or Camilla – who, by the way, should be the one to calm Cleo down and didn't even move to come and help poor Katie – could have handled Cleopatra any better. She's completely wild because her snooty owner never bothers with her."

The rest of the girls were all standing round with their mouths open. Jess was bossy sometimes, but they'd never seen her this mad. And she wasn't done! "And with both your faces stuck in a frown because you spend so much time looking down your big noses at people, how dare you even mention what anybody else looks like!"

"Well, I don't think I could have said it better myself!" a man's voice interrupted.

Red in the face and breathing heavily, Jess turned to see who had just heard her scream at Henrietta and Camilla . . . It was the gorgeous Will!

Chapter Seven

Jess was shaking. She hated arguing and was really embarrassed that such an important person had heard her. "I'm sorry . . . I—" she started, looking at the ground.

"Don't be," Will interrupted, smiling. "I *really* couldn't have said what you just did any better myself. And it sounds like it should have been said a long time ago!"

Jess didn't know what to say. A stunning, really famous actor was telling her it was OK that she'd just given someone a mouthful!

She looked up, blushing, and noticed that Carl was standing just behind Will too.

They must have come over together. Things were getting worse!

"*I'm* sorry for shouting at you earlier when I should have been grateful," Carl said, coming over to her. "You really saved the day back on the set, Jess, thank you. I'm only sorry that poor Katie got caught up in it."

Amber, Sam, Mel, Cara and Darcy finally closed their mouths. They couldn't believe that Will had stuck up for Jess, or that Carl was being so friendly – the nicest he'd been all day!

"You're *sooo* right!" said Mel, loudly enough for the two livery girls to hear. "Good one, Jess!"

Henrietta and Camilla said nothing, but they looked daggers at Jess and the two men.

Will ignored them and grinned at the director. "Carl," he said, "why don't you tell

Jess the reason we came to speak to her?"

"To me?" Jess squeaked, finally managing to say something.

Carl smiled at her. "Jess, honey. Any chance we could get your mum or dad here quickly? I'd like to speak to them."

"Mum's at home. She doesn't work on a Saturday so she can be around for Charlie, my brother." Jess was worried. Why would Carl want to speak to her mum? "Please, Carl. Don't tell Mum I lost my temper with Henrietta. I'll apologize to her and I promise it won't happen again."

'No way I'd make any promises like that!' she heard Sam mutter cheekily.

But Carl was shaking his head. "No, I don't think you understand. I'm not telling you off." He drew her to one side and lowered his voice so the others couldn't hear. Will followed too. "Listen, sweetheart," Carl said kindly, "I know it doesn't look like much, but it will change all the layouts and lighting plans if we have to lose a person and a pony at this stage. Katie's still waiting to be seen at Casualty and won't be back in time. I like sparky people, and you've just shown that you're not afraid to stand up for others – or for yourself. You saved the day back there and you're the same height and build as Katie . . . So . . ."

Jess held her breath. *Was Carl actually going to ask her what she thought he was?*

". . . I was wondering if you'd be prepared to stand in and take Katie's place. We—"

Jess didn't let him finish. *"Yes!!!"* she shouted, jumping up and thumping the air.

"Carl, Will, thank you so much. I'd love to be in the show!"

"What?!" the other girls shouted as they overheard Jess's outburst.

"I'll need to get your mum to sign health and safety papers and some other stuff to say that it's OK for you to appear on screen. But if she says it's all fine, then I'll take that as a yes, shall I?" Carl asked, grinning.

Jess was too shocked to speak: she just nodded – a massive smile on her face for the first time in ages.

"Amazing, babe! Well done!" yelled Amber, rushing over to give her best friend a big hug. The others crowded round to congratulate her too.

"You're gonna be famous!" yelled Darcy.

Sam shouted, "Whoo-hoo!" tripping over a yard brush in her excitement!

Henrietta and Camilla were not impressed.

"This is disgraceful," Henrietta snapped. "How on earth can that bossy, common little idiot go on TV with a beautiful pony like Cleopatra?"

"Actually," Camilla said snidely, "I don't want Cleo to be used for the filming any more. She's had enough of being handled by morons for one day. I don't give my permission for her to be used."

Jess's heart sank, and she saw Carl open his mouth to speak, looking absolutely furious.

But Will stepped up to the snooty girl and looked her in the eye. "Well," he said, "that, I suppose, is your decision." He looked as if he was going to walk away from her, but then turned back. "Oh, will your mum be seeing my Aunty Joan any time soon?" he asked calmly.

Camilla nodded slowly.

"Good. I'll be sure she knows how helpful her daughter's been today."

The stable girls grinned to themselves and Carl chuckled under his breath.

"Brilliant!" Amber whispered.

Camilla knew she was beaten. She fired another dirty look at Will and then snapped, "Whatever!" before grabbing Henrietta's arm and storming off.

"Oh, girls!" Carl called after them.

"Before you slink off, there's something you could do. Vicki said you'd be able to help out with whatever I wanted. There's quite a lot of horse muck in the yard now and it's spoiling the shots. Would you mind sorting it?" Then, without waiting for an answer, "Thanks! I knew you'd see it my way!"

Henrietta opened her mouth to argue, a look of disgust on her face. But Camilla stopped her. "Hen, I don't want Will to talk to Mummy. Let's just go." And they stomped off towards the yard, moaning to each other.

"Wait for me!" Will called, smirking. "I think I'll come over with you. Just to check the job's done to the standards I know Carl expects." He ran over and elbowed his way in between them, then linked arms with them. "Right, then. Let's go, shall we?"

"Good!" Carl smiled, turning back to the other girls, who were all laughing their heads off. "Now, let's get sorted. Jess, go and call your mum and see if she OKs this, then we'll send somebody to go and fetch her. We'll have to get you into costume and make-up too . . . Girls, would the rest of you mind awfully making these gorgeous ponies look as lovely as they did before, then hopefully we'll start again ASAP.'

With that, he grabbed Jess's hand and led her away from the stables, calling, "Thanks, darlings," over his shoulder as he left.

"This is all happening so fast!" cried Jess, smiling as she was led off to be a TV star. "I can't believe it!"

Chapter Eight

An hour later, Jess was in heaven! Her mum
and her brother, Charlie, had been just as
excited as her over her chance to be on TV.
Her mum agreed straight away and jumped
at the chance to meet her favourite actor!

Jess stood with them now at the edge of
the yard, wearing a blue hoodie and brown
jodhpurs from the costume department and
lots of strange make-up that made her face
feel like it might crack!

The yard girls led their ponies over, with
Susie leading Rose and Vicki leading Cleo.
Vicki wanted to make sure that Cleo was
calm before she met all the microphones,

cameras and lights again. She'd taken her for a quick gallop across the field to tire her out a bit. It seemed to have worked.

They arrived just in time to see Henrietta and Camilla scooping up the last steaming pile of manure from the yard into a wheelbarrow.

"I *so* have to get a picture of this!" laughed Darcy, taking out her camera phone.

"Smile, girls!" Sam shouted across at them cheekily. She looked over at Jess, who was still standing nervously with her mum and Charlie, and winked.

Jess grinned, and even her mum chuckled under her breath. "Maybe I should get my camera out too!"

"Right, darling," Carl said cheerfully, nodding at Jess. "Are you ready? We'll be moving quicker than before because the light's fading and I have to get this finished.

But do exactly what we've talked through
and you'll be brilliant.'

"OK!" Jess said, more confidently than
she felt. She walked over with the other
seven actresses to collect the ponies. It
was weird to walk towards Cleopatra
rather than her beautiful grey Connemara.

Jess really wished they could have been on TV as a pair. But she was excited and really proud of how well behaved Rose had been all day.

Cleo was behaving well now too. But, just in case, Jess spoke soothingly to her and walked her past the big microphones a few times so she was used to them being there. Then, heart thumping, she led Cleo over to her starting place, just in time for . . .

"Scene twenty-three. Take fifteen! Lights, camera, action!"

Time seemed to speed up. Jess did just as she'd been told. She led Cleo across the yard and had pretend gossipy conversations with the other girls. At first she had been tense in case Cleo played up. But the pony was being fine now, so Jess relaxed and started to enjoy herself.

In between every take, Jess looked over to her mum, who was taking photos, and

Vicki and the girls, who gave her a thumbs-up. Charlie kept sticking his tongue out. Jess was dying to laugh, but there was no way she was going to mess up this chance so she looked away quickly.

And then it was over! Jess was shattered when Carl called out, "And that's a wrap, girls. Thank you so much." He turned to the rest of the cast and crew and pointed to Jess. "I think a round of applause for our gorgeous heroine is in order."

Jess thought she was going to die of embarrassment as everybody clapped and cheered for her. Her friends cheered loudest of all, of course.

And Will whistled and whooped, making her blush.

She was shattered, but she'd hardly spent any time with Rose all day and wanted to get her sorted for the night. Mel offered to help Amber with the livery ponies so that Jess could take as much time as she needed with Rose.

When she'd got her make-up off and was back in her normal clothes, Jess walked over to the stables, smiling when she saw the ponies all in a row, with extra feed and hay because of the cold.

She gave Rose some warm bran mash to munch and some water to drink and spoke to her softly as she took off her saddle and bridle so she could brush her down.

An hour later, as it was getting dark, Vicki came in. 'Come on, babe, your mum and Charlie are waiting in the tack room with the others – there's some hot chocolate for you.'

Jess checked there was enough comfy straw bedding, hugged Rose for the last time and put on her stable rug to keep her warm. It was like a big pink duvet that kept Rose cosy during the night. "What an amazing day we've had, Rosie!" Jess whispered as she fastened the straps.

It had been amazing! Jess couldn't wait for her mum to get the photos she'd taken developed so she could stick them in her pony scrapbook. Will had even posed for one with her and said if they sent it to him when it was ready, he'd sign it for her!

"I'm really very proud, Jess, you know," Vicki said as they walked across the yard together. "I couldn't have handled that situation with Cleo any better myself. Katie's going to be fine too. Just a couple of stitches."

Jess blushed shyly. She idolized Vicki, so for her to say that meant more than anything.

"There's a bit of a surprise for you too, honey," Vicki added as they walked.

"Another one!" Jess laughed. "I don't think I can take any more today!"

"Oh, I think you'll like this one" – Vicki grinned – "but I'll let Carl tell you all about it."

Jess frowned. *What could it be? Why was Carl still here?*

As she entered the tack room, the girls were gossiping loudly, and Treasure and

Hunt, the stable puppies, were running
around, yelping noisily.

"Remember to wear old clothes
tomorrow, Car," Mel said to her best friend.
"Pete from the crew has given us the leftover
paint and there's loads of cool colours for
the ponies' stables."

"Oh, no," Cara said nervously. "What if I mess it up – I've never done any real painting before."

"Don't worry," Sam said, coming over to her. "I'm sure mine's going to be as messy as my clothes and my handwriting! We'll just all have to help each other."

Darcy stood in the corner, smiling.

"Wow, the whole school's gonna look different! And now that everything's so clean and tidy Vicki can concentrate on spending the money from the filming on replacing some equipment."

Just then, Carl noticed that Jess and Vicki had come in. He interrupted Darcy, "Of course, darling, you'll have to decide what you're going to spend *your* money on too," he said to Jess.

"What!" Jess screamed. *"Oh, my God!"*

"Now, don't get too excited," Carl said. "It's not much, and it's up to your mum whether you have it now or not, but it would definitely be enough for you to get yourself something nice."

Jess's mum gave her a big hug. "I've been so proud of you today, gorgeous. So it's great that you get something as well as the memories to show for it."

Jess looked around the tack room, her

pretty green eyes shining. All the people she loved the most were in one place and they were all happy. Jess felt like her heart would burst. She didn't have to think for more than a minute what she was going to use some of the money for.

"Well . . ." she started. "I think I'd definitely like to spend a bit of it on something new for—"

"Rose!" everybody shouted at the same time.

And Jess couldn't do anything but smile and nod!

THE END